To my little helpers, Jay and Ben.
Happy Christmas! Love Daddy
~ M. M.

tiger tales

5 River Road, Suite 128, Wilton, CT 06897

Published in the United States 2015

Originally published in Great Britain 2015

by Little Tiger Press

Copyright © 2015 Little Tiger Press

Text by Clement C. Moore

Illustrations copyright © 2015 Mark Marshall

ISBN-13: 978-1-58925-198-4

ISBN-10: 1-58925-198-9

Printed in China

LTP/1400/1154/0615

For more insight and activities,

visit us at www.tigertalesbooks.com

'Twas the Night Before Christmas

by Clement C. Moore

Illustrated by

Mark Marshall

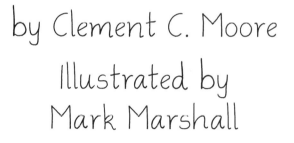

tiger tales

'Twas the night before Christmas,
when all through the house
Not a creature was stirring,
not even a mouse.

The stockings were hung
by the chimney with care,
In hopes that
St. Nicholas
soon would be there.

We children were nestled
all snug in our beds,
While visions of
s u g a r - p l u m s
danced in our heads.

And Mama in her 'kerchief, and Dad in his cap,
Had just settled down for a long winter's nap.

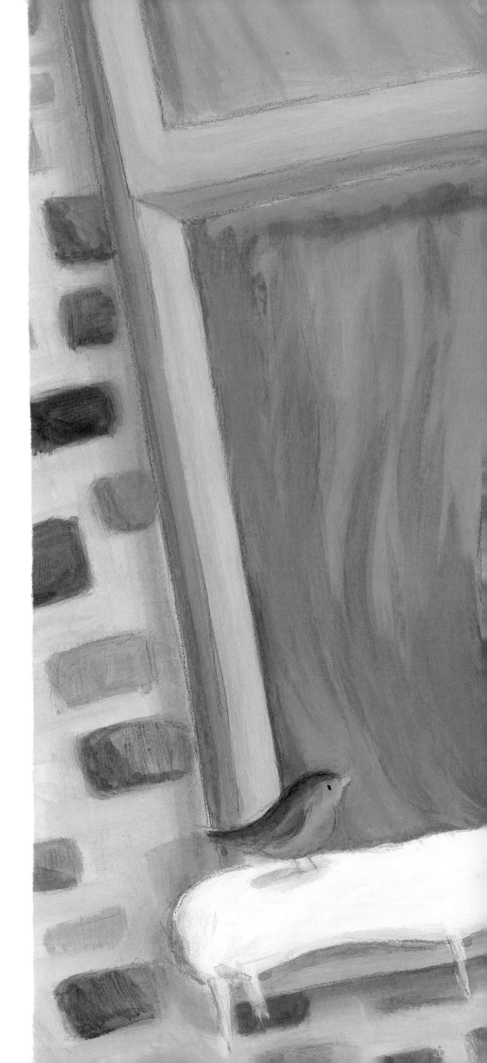

When out on the lawn
there arose such a
c l a t t e r,
I sprang from my bed
to see what was the matter.

Away to the window
I flew like a flash,
Tore open the shutters
and threw up the sash.

The moon on the breast of the new-fallen snow
Gave a lustre of mid-day to objects below.
When what to my wondering eyes did appear,
But a miniature sleigh and eight tiny reindeer,

With a little old driver so lively and quick,
I knew in a moment he must be St. Nick.
More rapid than eagles his coursers they came,
And he whistled, and shouted, and called them by name:

"Now Dasher, now Dancer, now Prancer and Vixen! On, Comet! On, Cupid! On, Donder and Blitzen!

To the top of the porch! To the top of the wall! Now dash away! Dash away! Dash away all!"

As dry leaves that before
the wild hurricane fly,
When they meet with an obstacle,
mount to the sky;

So up to the housetop
the coursers they flew,
With the sleigh full of toys,
and St. Nicholas, too—

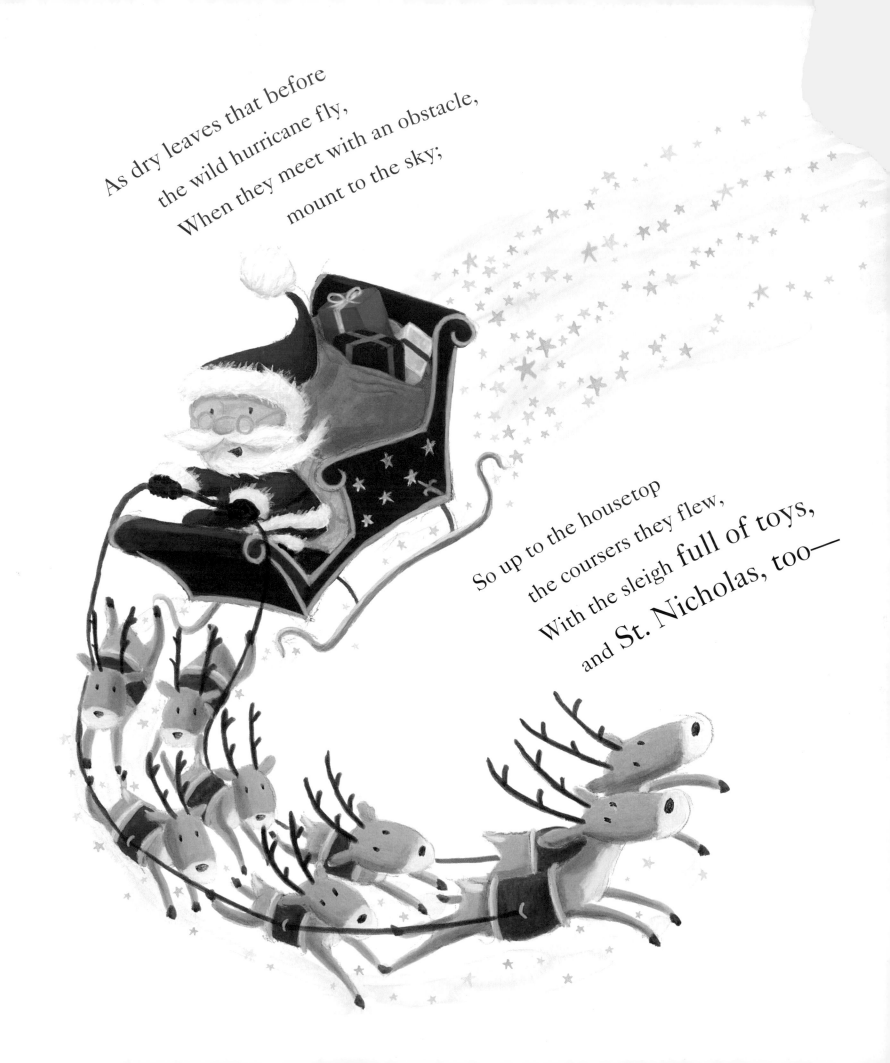

And then, in a twinkling, I heard on the roof
The **prancing** and **pawing** of each little hoof.

As I drew in my head, and was turning around,
Down the chimney St. Nicholas came with a bound.

He was dressed all in fur, from his head to his foot,
And his clothes were all tarnished with ashes and soot;
A bundle of toys he had flung on his back,
And he looked like a peddler just opening his pack.

His eyes—how they twinkled! His dimples, how merry!

His cheeks were like roses, his nose like a cherry!

His droll little mouth was drawn up like a bow,

And the beard on his chin was as

white as the snow;

The stump of a pipe he held tight in his teeth,
And the smoke, it encircled his head like a wreath;
He had a broad face and a little round belly
That shook when he laughed, like **a bowl full of jelly.**

He was chubby and plump,
a right jolly old elf,
And I laughed when I saw him,
in spite of myself.

A wink of his eye
and a twist of his head
Soon gave me to know
I had nothing to dread.

SAM

He spoke not a word,
but went straight to his work,
And filled all the stockings;
then turned with a jerk,

And laying his finger
aside of his nose,
And giving a nod,
up the chimney
he rose.

He sprang to his sleigh, to his team gave a whistle,
And away they all flew like the down of a thistle.
But I heard him exclaim, ere he drove out of sight—

"Merry Christmas to all, and to all a good night!"